Enjoy the

Happness

Cynthia Dennott

11/30/22

Mr. Bob's Corny Jokes

Cynthia Dewindt

Illustrated by
Raynald Kudemus
Illustrations inspired by Bobby Dewindt

To order additional copies of this book, contact:
Xlibris
844-714-8691
www.Xlibris.com
Orders@Xlibris.com

ISBN: Softcover   978-1-6698-4148-7
        Hardcover   978-1-6698-4495-2
        EBook   978-1-6698-4494-5

Print information available on the last page

Rev. date: 09/06/2022

Acknowledgements

I would like to thank Bobby Dewindt and his humor for making the story in this book possible. I would also like to thank my friend, April Harris for her colossal heart and unwavering support. A very special thanks to my daughter, Cynthia C. Avery and my sister, Judge Jessica Taylor. These two women have been a tremendous source of empowerment, love and inspiration, compelling me to be the best version of myself that I can be.

Cynthia Dewindt was born in Cheraw, South Carolina, in a small town called Patrick, population 250. Immediately following her birth, Cynthia's mother moved up North to New York City where Cynthia was raised with her three siblings. Although she was raised in the city, Cynthia's family has deep roots in the south, so she was exposed to the best of both worlds. As a health care worker, Cynthia values the importance of a pleasant smile and a good spirit. She is known for brightening the days of those in her charge. Mr. Bob's Corny Jokes is Cynthia's fi rst book. Although it is a children's book, it is also for the young at heart and is intended to put a smile on the faces of all who read it.

"Good morning, Dear," says Ms. Carol, as she stretched her arms out and opened the curtains.

Mr. Bob pokes his head out the bathroom door while brushing his teeth and said, "Good morning, Ms. Carol."

When Ms. Carol caught sight of her husband's face, she recognized that special look in Mr. Bob's eyes that lets her know that he was in his funny bone mood. At this point, she knew the house would be the opposite of quiet until he leaves for work.

"Do you plan to go to the market today?" yells Mr. Bob. "Yes, Dear. I'll be stopping by the market on my way home to pick up some soap along with some other things."

While Ms. Carol was yet speaking, an idea for a joke came into Mr. Bob's mind. Without wasting anytime, he said, "Honey, what did the soap say to the other soap?"

Ms. Carol's eyes looked toward the ceiling as she mumbled to herself the words: "Oh boy. Here we go!"

She answered, "I don't know, Sweetie. What did the soap say to the other soap?"

"You're all washed up!" laughed Mr. Bob. "Do you get the joke?"

"Yes, I got it," Ms. Carol said. Shaking her head from left to right, Ms. Carol thought of how corny her husband's joke was as she watched him laugh and laugh and laugh.

6

"I got a million of them," said Mr. Bob. "What did the toothpaste say to the other toothpaste?"

"I'm sure I don't know, Dear," she replied. "What did the toothpaste say to the other toothpaste?"

Laughing so hard and barely getting the words out, Mr. Bob said, "There's always something brushing up against me."

Ms. Carol watched her husband as he laughed at his own corny joke.

"Ahh, come on, Sweetie. You have to admit that was funny," said Mr. Bob.

"If you say so, Dear," replied Ms. Carol.

"It's six o'clock," says Ms. Carol. "I'm going to wake up little BJ for school."

At hearing this, Mr. Bob suddenly gets an idea for another joke. He follows her into little BJ's room and asked, "What did the clock say to the other clock?"

This time she doesn't respond so he just laughs and says, "It's about time!" "Ha, ha, ha, did you get it?" he said.

Ms. Carol just tilts her head and smiles so he said, "Ok, ok. That was a little weak. How about this one, 'What did the watch say to the other watch?'"

Without waiting for a response, he said, "You're taking a big wrist (risk). Get it?" he said, laughing at his own corny joke and holding his belly.

Sometime afterward at the breakfast table, Mr. Bob asked their son little BJ, "What did one deck of cards say to the other deck of cards?"

Little BJ guesses and says, "I don't know dad, 'let's play' I suppose."

"No," said Mr. Bob. "It said, 'Give yourself a hand.'"

To Ms. Carol's continued amazement, Mr. Bob and little BJ laughed at his corny joke.

Again he said, "Hey, BJ, what did the book say to the other book?"

Little BJ guessed again and said, "I don't know dad, 'if you read me, then I'll read you' I suppose."

"That's good, son, but no. It said 'You need to stop telling stories.'"

They both laughed some more. "Like father, like son," Ms. Carol thought.

This continued until they were all headed towards the door to begin their day out in the world.

17

Later that day, after finishing her errands, Ms. Carol gets in her car and heads home. Unfortunately, traffic was backed up on the expressway for miles. Ms. Carol and the other drivers could do nothing but wait.

As she sat there, she thought of what Mr. Bob might do to lighten the mood. He would probably ask, "What did the traffic light say to the other traffic light?" Then of course she would say, "I don't know." Then he would laugh and answer, "It would say 'this has got to STOP!'"

Ms. Carol smiled in her heart as she thought of the corny jokes her husband told earlier that day. Surrounded by so many frustrated drivers, Ms. Carol found herself laughing out loud while in a traffic jam.

As the cars finally began to move freely again, Ms. Carol's good mood continued. She thought of how grateful she was to be married to a man like Mr. Bob who works so hard to make her laugh by telling corny jokes and how she wouldn't have it any other way.

THE END

Printed in the United States
by Baker & Taylor Publisher Services